The Red Glass Ball

Touching Lives Through History

Linda Zeppa

Linda Zeppa

BOOK PUBLISHERS NETWORK

Book Publishers Network
P. O. Box 2256
Bothell, WA 98041
425 483-3040
www.bookpublishersnetwork.com

10 9 8 7 6 5 4 3 2 1

LCCN 2012936498
ISBN 978-1-937454-33-3

Editor: Julie Scandora
Cover designer: Karen Downing
Typographer: Leigh Faulkner

Contents

Forward

Be prepared to take a wonderful journey through moments in time as you experience the lives of others with each touch of a red glass ball. Wouldn't it be amazing if everything we touched in our life held a piece of that story for us? Linda Zeppa guides you through different times and cultures with *The Red Glass Ball* as her transport device. With each story you read, you will instantly feel that you have teleported right into the shoes of a stranger. And, by the end of each story, that stranger becomes a part of you. Linda's writing is compelling and transformative.

One thing that my life has taught me is that we have something to learn from everyone's story. *The Red Glass Ball* contains stories that will leave a permanent etching in your consciousness. From beginning to end, each step in this journey emotionally draws you in and unveils human motivations and insights throughout history. I found that by the end of the book, *The Red Glass Ball* had become an extension of humanity itself, posing the question to us: How many lives can we touch?

What traces of your life are you leaving behind? Each interaction, each glance, each shared experience is an opportunity for us to become like the red glass ball, leaving a lasting imprint on each individual. I hope that you will find each story as revealing and touching as the next, and somewhere in it all, perhaps *The Red Glass Ball* will leave its imprint on you.

Karen Downing
Spiritual Teacher at AurorasMessage.com

Acknowledgements

Thank you, *danke, merci, gracias, grazie*:

for the love, trust, and acceptance of my fabulous children, Katya and Matthew,

for the assistance and support of Karen and Aurora,

for the guidance, wisdom, and laughter of my friends and guides from the Margaret M Center for Intuitive Arts,

for the beauty and mystery of glass,

for the fabulous stories and pictures that lie within each of us.

Let me look into my crystal ball
to see what I can see.
Beyond the rosy haze there is
a world where all is free.
I gaze upon the scene
and offer you some knowledge
that you may leave or you may take
to free yourself from bondage.
I gaze upon the scene
and offer you a story
that you may take or you may leave
accept as pain or glory.

The Maestro

Giovanni leaned forward from his stool and peered into the flames of the furnace in front of him. The coals glowed yellow-red hot. In the center, the precious melt that he had concocted gently bubbled. The crackling of the flames around the coals seemed to rumble in the large quiet room. One by one, the other glassblowers had tamped or extinguished their furnaces and left. Now an hour after sundown, darkness embraced the workhouse around Giovanni. He was finally alone. It was not unusual for him to be there at this hour. He was Maestro Giovanni. The beauty, popularity and value of his creations gave him privileges not normally allowed. Working alone into the wee hours brought about much of his great work. The company lords and night watchmen, once skeptical, allowed and expected it.

This night was special, and he had planned it well. Several hours ago, as the others were putting the final touches to their work for the day, Giovanni had stoked his fire to keep it at a good moderate heat and began a batch. He worked diligently, completing other projects and preparing for the next, all the while keeping a close eye on this special batch. A bucket of fresh cold water stood close by. The wooden paddles, which he had formed himself, were arranged on the metal working surface to the right of the furnace. Beside them lay his tongs and two blow-pipes: one, the usual long iron rod; the other, a shorter and smaller *pontello*. All was ready.

For the last year, he had asked for and received small pouches of metal oxides to add to his batches. The resulting colors were awesome; they were planned, not just haphazardly appearing from residue in the sand. He favored the gold oxide—its crimson colored glass made his heart sing ... and the lords happy. Each time he had used it during the last year, he had scraped the last bits onto a small piece of cloth and saved them. He now had enough to make what he wanted. Reaching into the furnace with the long iron rod, he carefully scraped the scum from the top of the melt and stirred. Ahh ... it felt good. The frit was ready for the next step.

Giovanni gently stoked the fire again, turning the coals to ensure a high heat, crucial for the next step. Reaching below his stool, he took out the necessary ingredients, first, the small piece of cloth that, once opened, revealed the powdered gold oxide. To this he added a small bit of ash from yesterday's fire and a pinch of salt from the great sea. Barely breathing, he mixed the compound with his fingers. He took a tiny pinch of this substance, reached into the hot furnace, and sprinkled it over his batch. He repeated this twice more until the powder was gone. His hand was hot and burning, but he could think of no other way to keep his batch pure. His hands had become hardened from this work, and he would attend to them later at home in his small cottage.

This time, he took the metal rod to reach into the batch. He gently stirred and waited for the perfect consistency. At a precise moment, he twirled the rod through the melt, gathering up as much as he could in a large glob at the end. He pulled the rod from the furnace, grasped a paddle, and began to shape it into a ball. When ready, he reached for his pontello. This creation would not just be one hollow blown piece. It would also have small blown sections inside, yet be strong and perfectly rounded on the outside. As he concentrated on his work, everything around disappeared, and he became one with the mixture. Intuition told him when, what, and how to create this masterpiece.

Several hours later, Giovanni again reached into the fire, this time to tamp and ensure that it was safe to leave for the night. His tools and paddles were clean and back waiting on his work surface. Beside them lay his two creations. He gently touched the red bowl. Its shape was perfect, its surface smooth. It would catch a fair price, and the lords would be pleased.

Next to the bowl glowed his masterpiece, a perfectly round smooth ball, its' crimson color glinting in the light from the last embers of the fire. Looking into it, Giovanni could see small shapes and variations that he had carefully blown in. To the lords, these would be flaws. To Giovanni, they were perfection. "Ahhhh, yes," he smiled. "Perfect spots for secrets and dreams."

He picked up the ball, perfectly formed. The smoothness was comforting. It radiated a coolness that soothed his sore hands, yet also a warmth that touched his heart. It was heavy enough to make its presence known, yet light enough to carry anywhere. The radiant and varying crimson color drew him in, as if it was pulling the very thoughts from his head, the feelings from his being. Gently he placed it in his sack to take home.

"It is flawed to them," he justified, "but perfectly necessary for those like me."

Exhaustion finally hit him, and he made his way out into the night. The walk home was filled with thoughts of what this ball could be for him in the future ... a gift for a wife, when he found someone to love, or a ball for a daughter and son to play with ... or a means to leave this place and work on his own. For now, it would have a place of honor on the mantel in his small cottage.

The Crusades

Red ...

He saw the blood flowing from the body ... the fluid of life ebbing away.

"It's only nothingness now," he told himself. The life had left when the sword had pierced through the chest and heart.

The sword ... his sword ... taking a life.

It was his first kill. He knew that it was his duty as a Crusader, but it was a duty he abhorred.

Was there any other way?

"With peace," he gently heard through the thick air of the small cabin.

"Move on. It was meant to be. Remember this. The blood that spills now is for reasons known only to the souls ... from the past ... to the future. Yet take a memento."

An inner restlessness stirred him.

Quickly, as if by force, he reached over and grabbed a red glass ball from the mantel. It was heavier than it looked, but it fit easily in the satchel that rode over his shoulder. Taking a life was more than just flowing blood. It would never be easy for him.

His softly whispered "peace" seemed to resound through the room. With determination, he strode out the door to continue his elite religious duties.

The added weight of the satchel would be his constant companion through this life as a chosen soldier and warrior ... until he returned home.

The weight of the images in the red glass ball would be there forever.

The Silk Road

Rolling hills of sand stretched forever ahead, shifting and moving in beige brown curls and swirls and lines. Somewhere off in the distance, they met the blue of the sky. It was questionable as to where, for the horizon waved and glowed in the afternoon sun, forming a blend of what might or might not be there.

Xianzong gazed upon the scene. After three days in the desert, it still amazed him. The only changes were the size and shape of the unending sand. The sameness was haunting, the heat of the day oppressive, the cold of the night surprising.

One break in the monotony caught his attention. To the right, way off in the distance and just on the horizon, he could make out a land formation darker than the sand. At first he thought this was in his imagination. "The Tien Shan Mountains," one of the guides said. "It is best to keep them in sight at all times. They guide us along the north side of the desert and let us know we are moving in the right direction."

"Why not travel there?" Xianzong asked curiously.

"The route is hard. It twists and turns, and there are many bandits hiding among the rocks. The desert is better. Our route would be shorter if we could head directly across the desert," he continued seriously, eager to impress his client with his knowledge. "But the shifting sand and sameness of the Taklamakan confuses, and it is easy to get lost. Some never return. Wander forever."

Xianzong had plenty of time to think on this as the caravan moved forward. He walked alongside his camel, following those in front of him and leading those behind. All were loaded with supplies and provisions, many jugs of water, and wares of the merchants looking for trades ahead on the Silk Road. The packs on Xianzong's camel were stuffed with silk. He was a good merchant and had been excited to sell and acquire wealth, but now he wanted more. In the pouch tied to his waist, he carried a treasure that he had traded for at the market in Chang'an. It was beautiful. In the light, its red glass shimmered and glowed and moved while enclosed in a smooth ball shape. "Made only by special artists close to the sea. A special secret method," the trader had said.

Since setting eyes on this red glass ball, the urge to know how to make something so beautiful had driven him. Trading his silk at the marketplaces along this Silk Road no longer interested Xianzong. Instead, he was going to the end, somewhere by the sea, where he would trade his silk for learning the special secret method. His would return to Chang'an a glassmaker. His work would sell; he would teach others; he would make a great contribution to the Dynasty and receive much honor.

The snorting and stamping feet of the camel in front of him brought Xianzong back from his thoughts. Immediately, his camel began the same, as did each camel in succession behind him. The caravan came to a stop. Xianzong strengthened the grip on the reins and glanced up. In front, three of the guides were huddled, looking as agitated as the camels. One of them pointed ahead and to the left. Following his point, Xianzong was startled to see that the sameness of the horizon had changed. A large dust cloud had formed and was slowly moving across the desert. The wind, he noted, had picked up, and the sand was whipping up around their legs.

Small groups of men and camels converged along the route. The guides moved quickly from group to group, relaying information. Xianzong listened carefully, knowing that it was essential for him to understand. A sandstorm was heading in this direction. There was no time to avoid it. They must keep moving as quickly as possible until they could no longer move. Then they would rush to set up camp. Tents would be used today. Everything must be covered and marked. The camels would have to be unloaded and tethered. All men were to stay in the tents; no one was to wander alone.

As the guide moved on to the next group, Yinzong, a merchant making his third trip across the desert, assisted Xianzong and filled in the details. "We must keep moving as long as possible so as not to be completely buried as the whipped up sand settles," he explained. "The camels will not like it, so you must hold them tight and move forward forcefully and steadily. You are the boss of this animal brain. It will be hard moving. Pick up your feet and keep going until the stop order comes. You will see today how fast a camp can be set up!"

He showed Xianzong how to cover the lower part of his face with his *shemagh*. "I have been through this before. Do not fear. It will pass. Keep blinking your eyes as if you are

flirting with a beautiful woman. It will keep them clear. Ah ...
here we go now."

The caravan began to move. The wind gradually
whipped up faster, and the sand piled higher right before them.
Walking through the soft sand, almost dragging the reluctant
dromedary, was exhausting. The sun disappeared as sand and
dust swirled around. Xianzong could barely make out the camel
ahead of him when he finally heard the call to stop. All moved
quickly. The camels and men from behind advanced forward
and around and formed a circle. With much effort and yelling,
the skittish camels were lowered in order to unpack.

Xianzong's camel stamped and brayed as Xianzong at-
tempted to lower it. Trying to soothe the animal, he reached under and loosened the strap to one of the packs. His grip on the
reins loosened, and the strap slid from his arm. Eerily, with only
the sound of the wind in the air, the camel disappeared before
his eyes. It seemed to just drift off into the abyss of swirling sand,
and its braying dissolved with it. Xianzong yelled and moved
where it had gone but saw nothing; a few more steps and still
nothing. Looking back over his shoulder, he let out a loud yell
for help. Anger and upset over his lost goods turned to panic.
He saw only more of the abyss of swirling sand. All signs of the
caravan camp had disappeared. Even his footprints had already
been filled in. He turned his body around completely and stared
ahead. Was this the direction that he had come from? He was
alone in the midst of the violent swirl. His eyes burned with
sand and a desperate attempt to see through the fog. Dizziness
overcame him, and he closed his eyes. All was lost. He was alone,
confused, and incredibly sad. The whistle of the wind lulled him.
He felt light and airy, as if he too was a tiny particle, swirling

with the tiny bits of sand, each alone yet all moving together in perfect unison. A wild gust of wind caught him, and he slowly toppled forward, landing softly in the fresh drift of sand. As he fell, a heavy thud struck his upper thigh. The glass ball. His merchandise may be lost, but he still had this treasure. Loud roars of laughter erupted from his throat. He pulled himself up and took two steps forward. A voice called out, and a figure appeared before him. A guide reached for his arm and dragged him ten more steps forward into the circle of the caravan. "Crazy fool animal!" he yelled above the roar of the wind. "Did you not hear that no one was to wander alone?"

Xianzong wondered if the "crazy fool animal" was he or the camel, but had no time to ask. He was pushed toward a tent. "My camel ... my silk ... everything ...," he yelled desperately.

"You are lucky to be safe," the guide yelled back. "The things we will worry about later."

With a massive push, the man sent Xianzong flying into the tent.

• • •

The wind and sand whipped and roared outside for another hour that seemed like days. At times, it felt as if the entire tent would be picked up and all would be whirled into oblivion. The somber group sat or lay inside, dampened cloths soothing their stinging eyes. Each was alone in his space, yet swirled together in the midst of the storm. Then, as it had begun, the storm moved away. The noise lessened, the wind subsided, and silence overtook all.

Instinctively, the group made their way to the exit and stepped outside. The sun was low in the sky above the new rolling hills of sand, its heat almost unbearable. They had positioned the tent well. The entranceway had sand ankle deep, but the back of the tent had sand half way up, piled as if packed into the side of a hill. The camels, tethered to thick posts sunk in the sand, wandered around in front. Their heads bobbed as a signal for food and freedom. Several small mounds of sand encircled the camels. Scooping a handful off the top of one mound, a guide revealed the covering of one of the packs. Whoops, smiles, and relief filled the air, now empty of sand. "We have work to do," announced one of the guides. "The camels must be taken care of first, then do what is necessary for continuing our journey very early tomorrow morning."

Everyone moved into action except Xianzong. He wandered slowly out past the encampment. Inside of him, a storm of emotion swirled as violent as the sandstorm. Fullness and gratitude ... he was safe. Emptiness and sadness ... he had no camel, no goods. He still had the red glass ball, but now it was only a symbol of failure. The means for fulfilling his dream had disappeared into the sandstorm. He gazed ahead. The sun had set, and the air was cooling. The horizon was no longer hazy. Slowly, he turned around in a circle. It was all the same. There was no break in the monotony. They had lost the sight of the Tien Shan Mountains.

A guide appeared beside him. "I am off to look for your camel," he announced.

"But where ... how ... and—"

"Too many question!" he snapped. "I was tying down the right side of the tent when I heard your crazy laughter. I turned and took only ten steps before I found you. I will follow that direction over the new big hill and see what I can see."

"Can I go with you?"

"The desert is my life. I am better alone. Your help is needed here, and you must rest." Before Xianzong could protest, the guide was gone.

Time passed quickly. Fires had been lit, and the moon had risen. There was much to be done. Xianzong worked, digging the packs out from the mounds of drifted sand. He worked until exhaustion stopped his weary body and his chattering mind. He curled up in a corner of the tent and fell into a restless sleep.

Several hours later, he stepped outside the tent. The sun was just coming up, and the others had already been packing. Several were gathered together in a serious discussion. Which way should they go? With the mountains no longer visible to follow, each man had a different idea.

Xianzong turned his gaze beyond the right side of the tent. For the second time in one short period, a loud roar of laughter erupted from within. Coming up over the hill behind the tent was the guide, gently guiding the now docile camel, its head bobbing for food. From the left side of the camel hung one heavy pack. The others gathered in surprise around Xianzong. "Never thought that we would see that one again," Yinzong commented beside him.

Handing the camel reins over to Xianzong, the guide bowed deeply. "Thank you," he said reverently. "I am forever grateful."

Xianzong bowed back. "But I am the one who must thank you."

Raising his voice, the guide proudly made an announcement to all. "We wandered off in the blur of the sand yesterday. The search for this crazy beast has shown me where we need to go. We must travel for one half hour along the path that I have come. Then we will see the Tien Shan Mountains and turn west back on our path. Hurry before wind again covers my footsteps and those of this crazy beast."

Cheers and slaps greeted Xianzong and the guide as the men headed back to work. One brought feed for the camel. The guide stayed to help Xianzong balance the load on the camel while he ate. "You were gone all night. You must be tired."

"No," smiled the guide. "I found this camel after one hour of walking. He was braying loudly so I knew which direction to go for the last while. I gave the camel the bit of feed that I had brought, sat him down, and rested against him. I woke some hours later. It was then that I was able to see the Tien Shan."

He paused briefly. "I am sorry that we have lost one of your packs."

"I will have to make do with what I have left," Xianzong answered in a voice more reassuring than he felt.

"When we get to Kashi, I will point you to the places to make the best trades. Perhaps that will help." With a nod he was off to get the caravan moving.

. . .

To the right, way off in the distance Xianzong could again make out the land formations darker than the sand, the

Tien Shan Mountains. The caravan was back on track. His camel seemed happy; his load was lighter. Xianzong walked alongside his camel, following those in front of him and leading those behind. Physically, he was back on track, trudging along with the caravan. Internally, he had changed direction. His path would not be as he had planned. He would have to be wise and shrewd and accepting of help offered. Would he make it to the end of the Silk Road and the artists by the great sea? He knew not the answer. The future was as uncertain as the swirl of the sand in yesterday's storm. He would move one day at a time, one step at a time, one moment at a time. There was honor in that. He felt the weight of the red glass ball in the pouch at his waist. It spurred him on; he knew not why.

Rolling hills of sand again stretched forever ahead, shifting and moving in beige brown curls and swirls and lines. Somewhere off in the distance, they met the blue of the sky. It was questionable as to where, for the horizon waved and glowed in the afternoon sun, forming a blend of what might or might not be there.

Gypsy

"Please, Mama," Aishe begged sweetly. "Look into the ball for me. You do so for so many others and reassure them of their path. Look for me."

Kizzy smiled at her daughter. Even with her intuitive gifts, she was always surprised and awed by young people—especially her own fifteen-year-old. What had prompted this sudden interest and why now? "Help me set up my tables and wares, and then I will have time before the evening fair begins."

Routine set in, and Aishe pitched in to help. On the large folding table, she laid out the beautiful jewelry on the velvet cloth. The beadwork necklaces and bracelets, the bangles, all handmade by Kizzy and Aishe, shone beautifully in the late afternoon sun. Kizzy set up the small table. She lit the scented candle and placed it on the right side. On the left, she spread out the cards in a fan design. Old and faded, the cards still let their beauty and meaning shine through for Kizzy. They were family treasures, handed down to her from her grandmother. On the right, she placed a small iron stand. From a blue velvet bag, she took a beautiful ruby red glass ball and gently placed it on the stand. It seemed to radiate and hum as it fell into place. This ball and the cards held many stories and lessons for those who dared to pay and allow Kizzy to read what she instinctively saw within them.

Aishe had been restless lately. All of her fifteen years had been spent with her mother and this gypsy caravan, moving from place to place as the needs and whims of the group dictated. The group was her gypsy family. This wagon and tent were the only home that she had ever known. Yet she had always been a curious sort. She questioned where they were and why, wondering how others lived in one place all of the time, and eager to befriend those in the towns and villages. Kizzy smiled at her beautiful daughter and pointed to the chair across from her at the table. Both women, young and old, stared curiously into the ball. Kizzy was surprised by what she saw—a river in the background, a small house outside a village surrounded by gardens enclosed by a fence, three children playing in front of the house, and a woman sitting on the wooden stairs working with beads. It was apparent that the woman was Aishe. Kizzy looked up into her daughter's face and realized that Aishe had the gift—she also could read the ball and knew of the scene as well. "Wow," Aishe said softly. "It is beautiful but disturbing at the same time."

"Indeed," Kizzy answered in a voice that sounded steadier than her insides felt. "Always remember to follow your heart, no matter what the cards and the ball show."

"Yes, Mama. And I know that part of my heart will always be with you. I love wandering in this great wagon. And I love you!" She planted a kiss on her mother's cheek and jumped up. "May I go off now with my friends? We remember this town from last time and are planning a walk by the river to watch the sun set. Then we will be back for the music."

"Have fun!" Kizzy smiled as she waved her daughter off, feeling heaviness in her heart. Was it possible to change what she saw in the rosy glow of the ball? If they ignored it, would it go away? Was it possible to accept? What would life be like in the caravan without Aishe, and how would she manage in one place?

. . .

Three years later, Aishe walked along the same river. As before, the gypsies had set up the tables, ready for the evening fair. The town of Gaora had become a favorite for the caravan. The townsfolk accepted the caravan and its people, and so the gypsies returned twice each year, once in the spring and once in the fall, always abundantly supplied with wares and entertainment for the townsfolk. They enjoyed the music and dancing and counted on the caravan for their goods, jewelry, and services.

Aishe had her own reasons for calling Gaora a favorite. Her heart sang as she walked along the river, and anticipation filled her being as she drew nearer to the meeting spot. Memories of the last time here with John had filled her dreams, both night and day, for the last several months: the dancing and flirting, the secret smiles, the time alone ... and the passionate kisses. She had changed since then, grown in her longing. She missed him terribly and felt the eager yearning to share more physically and emotionally. That one person and one place—John and their spot by the river—could so consume her seemed rare and marvelous. This wonder and happiness caused her to distance herself from the sadness and concern in her mother's eyes, which, as the months passed, showed an acceptance as well. Aishe felt conflicted with this. Her mother was the greatest woman in the world and brought joy to her in the caravan community. Yet they both knew that adventure and a different world waited for Aishe beyond it.

Looking up from her thoughts, she saw him exactly where he was supposed to be, working on a building. When she called his name, he turned. Their eyes locked, and they made their way toward each other, joy and excitement coursing through their bodies. The two met in such profound energy that all else disappeared, and they became lost in their own space and time.

• • •

Tears flowed down Kizzy's face as she steered the wagon into place in the caravan line. She was alone for the first time in eighteen years. Aishe had not shown for the usual dawn leaving of the caravan, and Kizzy knew where Aishe was and whom she was with. She made no attempt to find her, as deep inside she knew that it was Aishe's place to be. It was easier for both of them if the caravan slipped away before Aishe realized they were gone.

Kizzy had the velvet bag in her lap. She reached inside and rubbed the ruby glass ball for the last time. Memories flowed through her: memories of a handsome man waving goodbye on an early morning as the caravan moved away, memories of Aishe's birth in the back of the wagon in another town far away.

Instinctively, she reached over the side of the wagon. As gently as possible, she dropped the bag at the side of the road and urged the horses forward. Her time with the ruby red glass ball was over. She no longer wanted its stories; the cards were enough. Her story was done, and they were moving forward as it should be. Choices had been made. She felt the love and trust of her beautiful daughter. Love would transcend time and distance. Trust would put them together again in the future.

Triangular Trade

Juan stepped briskly along the dock carrying the heavy keg with ease. His muscular body glistened with sweat in the warm afternoon sun as he swung the load over his shoulder and headed up the plank, leading to the bow and then down the stairs into the shadowy hold of the ship. This was the last of the cargo for the massive vessel in this port. Though still with room to spare, the hold would fill to overflowing, he was told, with a stop in Africa.

Anticipation and excitement coursed through his body, giving him extra energy to get this job done quickly. Fear of the unknown was squelched by the physical activity and list of things to do. Departure time from the Lisbon dock would be just past sunrise. That gave him this evening to see his family and say farewells before the adventure began. It would be at least a year before his return, and he was anxious to say his farewells properly. His father's illness had brought hardship to the family, and they would miss his labors, but the thought of the pay that he would return with made this choice acceptable. "Everyone will have to work harder," he thought. "But the money and goods I return with will help the family *tremendamente*. The stature of my farm family will change. With this and the many more voyages, I will bring much richness for us."

As he placed the keg down, the squelched fear rose up. He allowed it to take over while he stood alone in the shadowy hold. So much was unknown. Returning sailors barely spoke of these voyages. What should he expect of this, his first voyage? How would the family manage without him? Could his younger brother do the additional work? Would his father's illness overtake him during the long period of absence? Would Mari wait for him? He allowed himself a moment of pleasure as he visualized the beautiful Mari and felt the love that they proclaimed. Such a beautiful girl ... Was he a fool to leave her like this?

Approaching footsteps brought him back to the moment, and the worries again resumed their hidden spot within. "*Ah, bueno! Bueno!* Juan, you must go now. Enjoy your family for one last evening and see that beautiful young woman of yours." Marcos, the old shipmaster winked at him. "You must make memories to last a long sea voyage. But do not make such memories that will make you forget to be here on time in the morning."

"I wish that I knew more of what to expect," Juan confessed. "I like to do my best and fill my days. I feel that I have much to learn."

"All in good time," Marcos seemed to sigh. "Experience is the best teacher. Now be off. You must be here at sunrise to help us get out of this port and on with this. The sooner we start, the sooner we get back. I wish to return before I am a crotchety old man. This will be my last trip ... although, I said that last time as well. The promise of wealth keeps calling me, and I know not what I would do without the sea under my legs." He continued to mutter as he moved away, anxiously surveying the cargo.

Energy surged back into Juan, and he raced to get off the ship, through the dock area and city center to the quiet countryside beyond. He could make the half-hour walk in twenty minutes. The promise of a wonderful evening of family, friends, food ... and Mari quickened his pace.

• • •

The ship rocked gently as it slowly made its way into port, sliding quietly past the beautiful shoreline of sandy beaches and tree-lined bluffs. Under a clear sky, the sun beat down, illuminating the scene, sparkling the water, and reflecting off the spotless deck.

From the forecastle, Juan gazed at the foreign scene, a far cry from the bustling port of Lisbon. Here, silence reigned eerily over the harbor as they sailed toward a spot on a beach ahead. There was one long dock and what appeared to be an encampment just beyond it. The journey had been an easy one thus far ... almost boring. Two weeks of sun, calm seas, and a gentle breeze had guided them south to the shores of Africa. Now the sails and rigging were being rearranged for a day of different activity as they headed inland.

Juan had quickly managed to get his sea legs and fallen into ship life easily. The hard work of a farmer's son had trained him well. His job, he had learned, was to care for the cargo. He checked it several times a day, rearranging crates and barrels that had shifted or moved from the swaying of the ship. He helped to keep the hold clean and organized. "Save your energy," Marcos kept warning. "This is the easy part." But he would not tell more. "All in good time," he had said when asked for details.

With time on his hands, Juan had followed the others around on deck and learned. "Nosey Juan! Curioso Juano!" they called him. Nosey indeed—and keen to learn. He became aware of all that it took to move this great ship, the workings of the sails and riggings, and now felt comfortable anywhere on it.

The routine, the familiar, was about to change. He felt it ... an eerie expectation and uneasy rumbling deep in the pit of his stomach. The crew spoke little of the next step in the voyage. He had learned not to ask of it as it brought silence, a warning of discomfort best kept hidden. The only information he received came from the deck hands. The journey east across the Middle Passage would be long and hard, they had told him, where the winds blow up and change in the blink of an eye. It would take many weeks. "The next cargo will not be easy," Marcos had warned with foreboding in his voice. "It will move and squirm, and we will have to check it constantly."

· · ·

The next morning Juan watched in stunned amazement as the cargo made its way onto the ship. He had no heavy lifting to do—the cargo walked in on its own.

Last evening, the kegs and crates from Lisbon had been unloaded and closely scrutinized by the burly Englishmen on shore. They were eager to taste and test the refreshing contents of the kegs and partied late into the night, the ship's captain and his close workers willing participants. This morning, Juan, Marcos, and the five other crewmembers had loaded only a few crates of what appeared to be food. Then the captain had instructed them to watch the cargo carefully as it came aboard. "Our beer kegs have given us a wonderful exchange from the drunken Englishmen. Three hundred slaves!" he smiled greedily. "We must get all into the hold and quickly before they realize what a deal they have given us. The hold must be packed tight. Then we are off to the Americas and many riches! So much to barter with! Ahh, here they come."

He handed out long hard wooden sticks. "Not one is to escape," the captain ordered sternly. "Any attempt is to be stopped with a severe beating and a shove into the water. One example, and the rest will not try it."

With that he walked away to his cabin.

The cargo of slaves shuffled onto the ship. There seemed no need for the sticks. Heavy rope around one ankle of each tied them together. Heads were bowed down so as to carefully follow those in front. The rare look up revealed stunned expressions with eyes full of fear, anger, loathing, despair, questioning. The small bundles that they carried seemed soft and looked only to be a few extra garments. Their dark skin glistened. Was it from the heat of the sun, anxiety of the unknown, overwhelming fear, or all of it?

Juan felt the perspiration on his own body for the same reasons. His mind was racing in his stiff sweaty body. What was he doing here? This was not what he had expected. This cargo was people ... different from any he had seen before ... but definitely people. How would they all fit into the hold? How could they look at him with such loathing? They did not know him, as he did not know them. Where did they come from, and where were they going? Questions he knew that he could not ask anyone around. "Your job is to take care of the cargo," he sternly told himself. His hand gripped the hard wooden stick, knowing that he could never use it as the captain had directed.

. . .

Juan sat in the soft chair and stared blankly across the desk at the captain. Months had passed; he knew not how many. Physically, he had grown gaunt and pale; emotionally, sad and beaten; mentally, confused but still alert. He listened intently as the captain spoke. Before entering the captain's quarters, he had been determined to speak his truth. He now knew the impossibility of that.

"Curioso Juano!" the captain seemed to bellow. "I hear that you are a good worker, strong and determined ... and intelligent!"

"*Si, Capitan*. I am eager to learn."

"Then here is for you to learn. It is very unpredictable at sea, and you will be told this only once." He reached into his desk drawer and pulled out an object, dropping it with a loud crack onto the desktop. The noise startled Juan, and his body jerked. He recognized the object immediately—the red glass ball. It had been bright and shiny when his father had given it to him in Lisbon those many months ago. It seemed dull and heavy now. "Is this yours?"

"*Si ... pero, no,*" Juan stumbled over the words.

"*Si? Pero, no?* It is as I thought. The slaves who stole it from you have been punished. They will not take things again, and you will not see them again. You must be more careful with your things."

"NO!" shouted Juan jumping up from his seat. Words flew out of his mouth. "They did not steal it. I gave it to them. They will need it when we get to the Americas. When the selling begins, they can buy themselves and be free. They are good people who want a future. It must be so ... I know from speaking with them. I trust—"

"You cannot trust the slaves!" the captain shouted back. "They had what did not belong to them, and for that they have been taken care of. Perhaps you are not as intelligent as they say. Sit down."

Juan sank back into the chair and into himself. He dared not speak or think of what had happened. He obediently sat and listened. The captain lowered his voice but spoke with force. "You will no longer care for the cargo as you have. You will clean out and scrub the hold when the cargo is out with the others."

"*Si, Capitan.*" Juan gave the expected nod.

"We will arrive at our destination soon. You will stay on board and clean more. I do not want to see you near the cargo. Nothing more is to interfere with its sale. You have cost me two. That is more than I usually tolerate."

With a fierce look, he grabbed the red glass ball. It fell with a loud "thunk" back into the deep desk drawer. "Go, Curioso Juano," the captain ordered coldly. "But remember ... you cannot buy freedom. It is a long voyage home, and the sea is unpredictable, especially for those who are too trusting and stupid."

Somehow Juan made his way out onto the deck. The sun had set, and a warm breeze was blowing. He made his way to the bottom of one of the large masts. Fear and guilt overcame him. What had he done? What could he do now? He stood in the dark where no one could see the tears and the shaking. Marcos found him hours later and gently led him away. "It is time for your shift in the hold, my friend. There is nothing that hard stinky work will not cure. Don't worry. I will see that you get home. The hardest part of this long voyage is almost over. We will make it back. Trust me."

.   .   .

On a beautiful sunny summer day two years later, Juan watched from the edge of the field as a familiar figure walked toward him. It seemed to rock as it approached, swaying from side to side as it firmly stepped forward. A flood of memories crashed through Juan as the figure approached: the beauty of ocean waves and shoreline, the weariness and satisfaction of good physical work, the stench of the hold of a ship packed too full of human cargo, the fear in the white eyes and dark faces, guilt and remorse for being a part of something so barbaric. These painful memories haunted him daily and caused many a nightmare.

"Ah, Marcos, my friend!" Juan smiled and greeted.

"Wonderful to see you, my friend!" Marcos firmly clasped Juan's outstretched hand in both of his own. "Look at you! A happy farmer and, I expect, a hard-working one as well. Captain of your land!"

"Si! Si! It is hard work, indeed, but nothing that I cannot do. And I have a great crew." Juan gestured to those working in the field. His two younger brothers waved, and his beautiful wife, Mari, nodded and watched warily. "What brings your sea-faring heart so far inland?"

"My ship is sailing off next week, and I need help."

"No! No! I will never—"

"Never say never!" Marcos interrupted with a smile and spoke quickly. "Times are hard here. We can help each other. I hear that farmers are in need, and I am in need of trusting workers on my ship."

"Your ship?" Juan questioned.

"Yes!" answered Marcos proudly. "There was a mutiny on the last voyage. No need for details; you can imagine them." He reached into his bulging pocket, pulled out the red glass ball, and handed it to Juan. "I believe this is yours. I am now captain ... for one last voyage."

"Ah, Captain Marcos." Juan rubbed the smooth surface of the ball with his rough farmer hands and gazed into it. The memories in it strengthened his stance. "For you, there is always one more last voyage. I have had my one and only last voyage."

"But the pay will be excellent. You will be set for life. Under my guidance, the ship will be different."

"And your cargo?" Juan asked quietly raising his eyes to meet Marcos's. "I hear that many countries are banning the trade of slaves."

"There are still ways to get around that. Slaves bring the most profit, even more so with the ban. But we can arrange the cargo differently so that it is more pleasant. Besides, you will not have to work in the hold as the captain's mate."

"Still no. I cannot do it. I am settled and happy here. The memories of my last voyage are enough."

"You would have not made it from your last voyage if not for me. You trusted me. Now I need a trustworthy mate with me." Marcos paused and glanced out across the field. "If not you, perhaps one of your brothers?"

For several seconds an uneasy silence hung between the two men, a silence filled with tension and expectation. Reaching forward, Juan took Marcos's hand and firmly placed the red glass ball into it. Marcos looked confused. "But this is yours."

"Now it is yours," Juan answered firmly. "I have just bought freedom for me and my family. Good luck on your last voyage, Captain Marcos."

He turned and began to walk through the field. He felt light and free. He would never understand this concept of slavery. He saw only people on their own paths. His gaze rested on his family. They seemed happy and content to work with him. Their skin, like his, was dark brown, baked from hours of work in the sun each day. "A few shades darker," he chuckled to himself, "and we could be considered cargo."

Germany

Early evening on a cold January day, Papa returned from one of his meetings. He was more agitated than usual, and incredible sadness showed in his drooping body. The fear he tried to hide showed only in his dark eyes, which avoided directly meeting those of his loved ones. He spoke in a quiet calm voice. "We must leave. Immediately."

Everyone sat frozen for several minutes. During the past few months, they had known of several families who had simply disappeared. It was "for their safety," the children were told. Some families went with the soldiers in their great cars. Others slipped away during the night without saying goodbye. It was never expected to happen to them, such a good family. Instinctively, Mama took over, speaking to the three stunned children in a strong voice. "*Mein kinder**, listen carefully. Get your large rucksack and fill it only with essentials. A change of clothes. Two pairs of socks. A notebook and some pencils. A few of your special treasures that fit and one small toy. You must be able to carry the rucksack a long way, so choose lightly. If you still have room, you can carry something for me. Now, hup, hup! You have five minutes."

*kinder-children

"Dress warmly," Papa added. "Two layers of clothes and your warm boots. It is a cold night, and we have a long way to walk."

As ordered and with none of the usual bickering, the three children moved quickly in the only bedroom that they had ever known. The large room, affectionately called "*kinder'a zimmer*," had space along one wall for the beds and belongings of the two boys. Separated by a heavy curtain was an alcove where ten-year-old Mia had her own space as the youngest and a girl. Mia tried to think through the haze in her mind—two pairs of socks, undergarments, a shirt ... Her eyes wandered to the beautiful red sphere on the table near her bed. As she reached for it, her brother's head appeared around the curtain and his voice cut through the haze. "You are not taking that. It is not essential, and it is too heavy to carry. Why don't you take that little *puppe*** on the bed?"

"But Oma gave this to me. It is a treasure, and I might need it." Mia's voice was trembling but stubborn. Thirteen-year-old Walter spoke back more sharply than he intended, and stronger than he felt. "It will be heavy. Just remember, I will not carry your bag for you. I have my own. Take the *puppe*."

As he turned away, Mia firmly grasped the red glass ball. It was smooth and warm and sent a gentle wave of calm assurance through her hands and into her heart. She remembered Oma's words. "There is magic in this ball. The red gives you courage. The glass gives you strength. Let it remind you always of your own power, my dear Mia. You are Mighty Mia!" She rolled the ball in her sweater and placed it in the top center of her rucksack. It would balance out the load. She continued to

***puppe*-doll

dress in warm layers. The five minutes had passed, and she had to be ready.

• • •

Obershutze Franz walked briskly beside his comrade through the dark streets toward the edge of town. It was close to midnight, and it had been a long day. As a young soldier, he had learned quickly to do exactly as told, to follow the call of the führer and show a strong face, especially when in uniform. The regimen exhausted him, physically and mentally. Attention was required at every moment and to every detail. A second of inattentiveness could prove costly. No dreaming allowed! As they approached a corner, his companion slapped him on the back and smiled. "We are lucky to get this little break away, even for such a short time. Home is such heaven after the noisy barracks. Enjoy what is left of the night with that lovely bride of yours." Then he turned serious. "Remember we must serve again at noon. The morning will come quickly. Do not be late. *Gute nacht*."

Finally, Franz was alone with his thoughts. He breathed in the stillness, peace, and quiet of the winter evening and picked up the pace, anxious now to reach home for this short night. A little time was better than none. He was grateful to be stationed close by. With luck, his mother-in-law would already be asleep, and the night would be for him and Maria! Ah! Such blissful thoughts! Another fifteen minutes and he would be there.

Muffled noises interrupted his thoughts, and he glanced up. Soldier skills instinctively kicked in, and he analyzed the area in front of him carefully. Barely visible in the shadow of the trees at the very edge of the road were moving figures. Curfew was in effect, and only soldiers and permitted people were allowed out at this time. It was his duty to investigate. Quietly, he removed his weapon from under his heavy coat. As trained, he stealthily moved behind them to a distance of three meters and spoke out clearly. "Halt! In the name of the führer!"

Startled gasps rang out, and the figures stopped. "Come out of the shadows into the moonlight and show your papers," he ordered, keeping his weapon in full view. The situation was easy to assess. Five figures, obviously a family and obviously fleeing, stepped slowly into the lighted roadway. The largest, the man began digging through his bag for the non-existent paperwork. "This is a cold night to be out for a family stroll. Where are you off to?" he asked casually.

The woman answered confidently. "We are off to see my mother in Gerstadt. She is ill and needs my help. Besides, it is best to get the children out of the town and into a quiet village with all that is happening."

"It might be best for the children to be sleeping on a cold night and traveling by day. You are aware of the curfew. Now where is the paperwork?" Franz's tone was harsh. What was wrong with these people? Could they not have waited until tomorrow? He could not bring himself to shoot them as other soldiers would. Therefore, he was obliged to bring them back to headquarters, guard, interrogate, file paperwork, and follow more orders. His night off was ruined.

Knowing that the proper paperwork did not exist, Franz accepted the envelope from the man while avoiding his eyes. It was easier for him to deal with situations such as this when he did look at any human factors. He could then be ruthless and carry out his duty as a soldier and enforcer of the laws and rules of the nation. The envelope held money—many marks—and a sheet of paper with the single word, "*Danke*," on it. "Nice," he said to the silent faces, "but not the type of paperwork that I was looking for."

"Great," he thought to himself. "Now I must add bribery to my list of complaints."

His anger spurred him on. He concentrated on the man in front of him. "Is this all? Is your family not worth more than this?" he snarled. "And what other treasures do you have to offer me?"

Startled and fearful now, the man tried desperately to look Franz in the eye, keeping his gaze away from the rest of his family. "We have some jewelry and family treasures. It is imperative that we get to Gerstadt. Surely you understand our paperwork and can be of assistance."

Sensing movement, Franz moved his weapon in that direction. It was pointing at the smallest member of the group. A young girl had moved within his reach. Her eyes looked up at him, and her hands reached up to offer him something. "Here," she spoke quietly and firmly. "Here is a treasure—magic and power beyond belief."

Instinctively, he reached for what she offered. It was heavier than he had expected it to be. At first, he thought that it was a round stone, but it felt smoother and warmer in his gloved hand. He held it up to the moonlight. A radiant red haze shone through it. He was mesmerized by the color and dreamy quality. In the midst of the haze, a picture took shape. A steaming bowl of soup and a refreshing beer lay in his spot at the kitchen table. Maria sang softly as she cut slices of bread at the counter. She stopped and stared back his way, meeting his eyes. Her hand gently rubbed her stomach and she smiled expectantly. A feeling of love and urgency overtook Franz. He lowered the ball and looked around.

He was alone. The family was gone. He knew that they could not have wandered far and that he could easily overtake them. Guilt ran through his soldier's mind. He had allowed himself a few seconds to dream. But his sense of urgency was not of the soldier's nature; desperately, he needed to get home. He glanced again at the red ball in his hand. What a wonderful gift it will be for Maria! What would she see in it? He placed it gently in his pocket with the envelope, returned his weapon to its usual spot and moved toward home. "If I run, I can be there in five minutes."

• • •

The family moved quickly and quietly. They continued to follow the road but stayed completely in the protection of the trees on the other side of the ditch, although the going was more difficult as the snow was deeper and there was no path. They barely dared to breath. Finally, Papa stopped and motioned for the others to gather close. From her pack, Mama pulled a thermos and offered a soothing drink of strong tea to everyone. In a hushed voice, Papa said, "The farmhouse we are headed for is just over that hill. We should be there within the hour." With that he turned and again set the pace.

Turning to follow, an exhausted Mia stumbled. A reassuring hand reached and grabbed her rucksack, holding her up. As she moved forward, the rucksack was taken off her shoulders as Walter's voice whispered in her ear, "You are courageous and strong beyond words, Mighty Mia. I am grateful that you did not bring the puppe. Your bag is easy for me to carry." He slung it over his shoulder to join his own and gently guided her forward.

The Present

The first rays of the rising June sun slanted through the trees, sparkling on the dewdrops, soaking into the damp grass, and steaming the fresh dark mulch around the brilliantly colored flowers. Soft chirping and chattering broke the silence as the birds, young and old, greeted the day and each other.

I moved quietly and carefully so as not to disturb the scene or attract the attention of the others inside. The scent of the fresh morning air hit me as the screen door opened. I shuffled slowly across the cool slate surface of the small patio. Gently, my tired achy body and the treasure that I carried cradled in my lap sank into my favorite chair. I soaked in the beautiful morning, letting the early sun warm me and soothe the soreness.

My eyes drifted to what lay in my lap. The sun made it brilliant, and today it especially radiated a ruby red, reflecting a soft halo of crimson shadow. My searching hand felt the warm smooth surface, soothing the uneasy feeling within me. A calm reassurance and peace flowed through my body and soul as I stared into the red glow. Far more than a red glass ball, this was indeed a treasure.

I had written instructions and left them with my belongings. When I was gone from this earthly plane, the red ball would be with my granddaughter Lily. She was the one who knew its beauty and magic. She was the one who held it as a treasure. She was the one who saw all that was in it and of it. Yet I sensed that the form of the ball was about to evolve in a transforming universe. As an intuitively gifted artist, Lily would change something about this ball.

•   •   •

"Gramma, this feels so good," she had gushed last weekend. She had come home from college for the weekend. "I sure needed a break away from it all, and I knew I would find it right here."

I watched as she lovingly cupped the red glass ball in her pretty young fingers and gazed into it. It was always the first thing that she reached for in the room after the usual cheek kissing and hug. She plopped down on the chair beside my bed. It was early evening. My tired body relaxed in her soft energy even as my sharp mind knew that she had come to see me one more time. "I never tire of your stories, Gram. You have shared so many with me. I always come and sit with this beautiful treasure. It makes your stories seem so real. When I was young, I would play with it. Now I just find such peace sitting with it in my lap, just as you have for years. I feel that the stories are hidden within it. Where did it come from?"

"My father, your great-grandfather, brought it back for me when he returned from the war. He said that it came from Germany. He would not tell me how he got it. Looking at it gave me peace as well; but it made him uneasy. It reminded him of the war and fighting ... and I suppose blood as war spills much of it. So I kept it in my room."

"What was he like?" she asked.

"He was different when he returned from the war," I answered honestly. "His outward nature had turned in. Loud noises bothered him, so I became a quiet child in his presence. He got his job back at the mill. During the war, women worked at the mill, but they were all let go when the men who returned needed their jobs back. He spoke of his job very little. It appeared dull and boring and meaningless to him. During evenings at home, he was quiet and sullen. Three or four times a week, he spent time at the hall with the other veterans from the war. That seemed to be his only enjoyable time."

"What did they do at the hall?" she asked. "Did you go with him?"

"They played cards, drank beer, and talked of things that no one else seemed to understand. At first, I was too young to join in. Sometimes, my mother would send me to get him and help him home. We would giggle and joke as he stumbled his way home. As I grew older, it was not as much fun. He embarrassed me with praise in front of his friends. There was less giggling on the way home, and his jokes became incoherent. Sometimes, I was the one stumbling as I half carried him home. And then we had to face the wrath of my mother. While I was dragging him home, she prepared great meals and great tongue-lashings."

"Was he an alcoholic, then?"

"I don't know. We never thought of it that way. In those days, it was just accepted that some men drank, especially those who had made it back from the war. I never thought of him as sick or a drunk. I just thought of him as my father who needed some sort of escape from something unknown to us that he had trouble living with.

"I remember so clearly the last time that I stumbled home with him. It was my last week of school. I was starting a new job as a secretary in the offices at the mill. He was very proud of me but also very sad. For the first time in a long time, I understood what he said. He told me that I had a gift. I must look into the red glass ball and see the stories of love. The stories of war were deeply hidden within where they could hurt no one and would surface only if needed to teach us peace. I had already felt much of the magic of this ball, and I reassured him that it brought me great joy and peace."

"What happened to him? " Lily asked tentatively, aware of some sadness in my voice.

"As he stumbled home alone one night the following winter, a car lost control on the icy road and hit him on the sidewalk. He never regained consciousness and died a few days later."

"Oh, Gram! How sad!"

"Yes and no," I answered. "He had lived too long with his buried stories, and it was time for him to move on from this life. He left me ... or us ... with the many stories of the red glass ball and the opportunity to add our own."

"I understand," Lily sighed. "Acceptance and change are so difficult. Life seems so hard at times. For me, it is hard to grow up, be who I need to be and find my way as an adult in this world. It would just be nice to sit here with the comfort of this warm red glass in my lap and live in the stories it tells."

"Live your own story, Lily, as it is meant to be. Trust and know that it will be a great one. Take what is special from the stories shared and begin anew. It is time for a new beginning. We need the wisdom of the old with the power of the new." I pointed to the ball in her lap. With a twinkle in my eye and a smile on my lips, I added, "It does not always have to be serious, you know. Now fill me in. Tell me about the concert that you went to last week. Was the band loud enough? Was there a mosh pit or whatever they call it? Did you get moshed?"

Lily's eyes sparkled with tears and laughter as she started her story. "I can't believe that I tell my eighty-year-old Gramma my crazy adventures, and she actually enjoys them ... without getting all worried and in a flap. What will I ever do without you?"

· · ·

On another beautiful June day, family and friends gathered on the small patio and spilled onto the gardens beyond to pay respect to Gramma Beth who had made her transition to that special place beyond this earthly dimension. A whirlwind of feelings and emotions floated around: relief that her physical pain was over, sadness for what many believed to be an unfulfilled life, loneliness for the intimate conversations and understanding that each had experienced so many times, uncertainty over what would become of this place that seemed to hold them all together.

Lily stood in the midst of this whirlwind, different from those around. She took in all of these emotions yet wanted more. She sensed Gram there, smiling, and again heard her words, "We need the wisdom of the old and the power of the new" and "It does not always have to be serious, you know." Lily wanted to feel joy and felt the urge to somehow bring shock and laughter into this mix. This was not the end of Gram. This was the new beginning.

Lily reached into her bag and took out the red glass ball. She had kept it within reach since Gram had passed, and it had given her great comfort. But she knew that Gram had entrusted it to her for a much higher purpose and now she needed to act. Her eyes twinkled as Gram's had, and she smiled as broadly as Gram had. In a clear voice, she spoke, "Thanks, Gram, not only for your wonderful life but for the many that you shared with your stories and tales. Here is to the wisdom of the old and the power of the new!" With that, a great force took hold of her hand, and the ball flew up high above the crowd. With a fabulous crunching sound, it hit a branch of the great oak tree above. The red glass ball shattered into millions of tiny pieces as fine as ash, sparkling and drifting in the bright June sun. People moved everywhere, avoiding or catching the tiny bits that gently floated down. The fear of injury quickly disappeared, and laughter and joy ensued. It seemed a beautiful dance. "Gramma's own mosh pit!" laughed Lily.

• • •

Lily returned to the patio after everyone was gone, carrying a broom, a dustpan, and a bag. Quietly she began to sweep the fine ash and tiny glass pieces from the slate surface of the small patio. A pile formed, and she swept that onto the dustpan and then reverently poured it into the bag. Her intuitive creativity was kicking in again. She could use this in the glass studio at school to start a new glass something. Would it be a ball? Would it be red? She was not sure, but she definitely knew that it was going to be a very special treasure ... something new mixed with the remnants of the old. A new beginning indeed!

The New Glass Ball

Lily made her way through the main entry of the old building and followed the signs for the main gallery. The refreshing and cool hallway gave a welcomed reprieve from the hot sun of this Italian mid-morning. Her artistic eyes drew in what surrounded her—paintings and drawings, sculptures and glassworks, ancient and modern, all reverently displayed in a centuries-old building.

She had arrived early and alone this morning. Her artistic creation, "The New Glass Ball," was on display here, in the glassblowing capital of the world, as part of a world tour. Tonight she would attend the reception, which would honor her as a Maestro. Before that, she wanted to see it on display for herself, anonymously mingling with the crowds, and feel what was causing such a stir.

The large main gallery displayed several other glass pieces along the walls, but the focal point of the room was "The New Glass Ball." About a foot in diameter ("thirty-three centimeters," the brochure read), it sat on a pedestal in the center of the room, enclosed by a velvet rope. Lily recalled its heaviness, still wondering how she had had the strength to maneuver it during its formation. Somehow, instinctive and intuitive motions had governed her work. It had been created through her, she knew not how. It just was. As she moved around the back of the small crowd, rays of muted sunlight came through the skylight above and hit the ball. She gasped, paused, and gazed deeper.

She had not laid eyes on this treasure for a while as it had been on tour for several months. In the interim, its beauty seemed to have deepened. The colors swirled within ... the red remnants of the old red glass ball and all the colors that she had been driven to add ... cobalt, emerald, orange, yellow, purple ... and combinations of some and all. They were all there, swirling and twirling as if still liquid, yet perfectly solid and stable together. Energy flowed through her. She felt first the red, warming and stirring and filling her with memories—and then allowed the other colors to sweep up through her. She was emptied and then refilled. Warmth, peace, and knowing overcame her, just as they had while making this treasure.

Yet "The New Glass Ball" had changed since then. It had aged and seemed to have collected more on this tour it was on. In return, it was emitting a peace, strength and wisdom to anyone who gazed upon it, receiving and giving power. This was not just her masterpiece; it was one for the world.

Her trance was broken by the soft-spoken words around her.

"*Magnigico!*"

"*Maestoso!*"

"Wow!"

A child's voice reached above the rest. "Look!" the young voice cried excitedly. "There are all the colors of the world! All mixed together but by themselves. It makes me feel good!"

The warmth, peace, and knowing within Lily deepened. She felt that it was for everyone else who gazed upon this treasure, for it held within it the wisdom of the old with the power of the new. A new beginning ...